Horse

Snake

Sheep

Dragon

Monkey

For nearly 5,000 years, the Chinese culture has organized time in cycles of twelve years. This Eastern calendar is based upon the movement of the moon (as compared to the Western calendar which follows the sun's path). The zodiac circle symbolizes how animals, which have unique qualities, represent each year. Therefore, if you are born in a particular year, then you share the personality of that animal. Now people worldwide celebrate this fifteen-day festival in the early spring and enjoy the start of another Chinese New Year.

Rabbit

Rooster

Tiger

Dog

Ox

Pig

Rat

To Randy, Amy, Lucas, and the Lau family:
for the dear horses who've accompanied me in every stage of my life.
—O.C.

For my wonderful grandparents who paved the way and made such an influential impact and to every teacher and mentor who inspired, encouraged, and motivated me as I took the reins on my artistic journey.
—J.W.

immedium

Immedium, Inc.
P.O. Box 31846
San Francisco, CA 94131
www.immedium.com

For information about special discounts for bulk purchases, please contact
Immedium Special Sales at sales@immedium.com.

First hardcover edition published 2014.

Edited by Don Menn
Book design by Erica Loh Jones
Calligraphy by Lucy Chu

Printed in Malaysia
10 9 8 7 6 5 4 3 2 1

Library of Congress Cataloging-in-Publication Data

Chin, Oliver Clyde, 1969-
The year of the horse : tales from the Chinese zodiac / by Oliver Chin ; illustrated by Jennifer Wood. -- First hardcover edition.
pages cm
Summary: "Hannah the horse befriends a boy named Tom, as well as some other animals of the Chinese lunar calendar, and demonstrates the qualities of a brave spirit. Lists the birth years and characteristics of individuals born in the Chinese Year of the Horse"-- Provided by publisher.
ISBN 978-1-59702-080-0 (hardcover) -- ISBN 1-59702-080-X (hardcover)
[1. Horses--Fiction. 2. Courage--Fiction. 3. Animals--Fiction. 4. Astrology, Chinese--Fiction.] I. Wood, Jennifer, illustrator. II. Title.
PZ7.C44235Ydp 2014
[E]--dc23
2013001008

ISBN 978-1359702-080-0

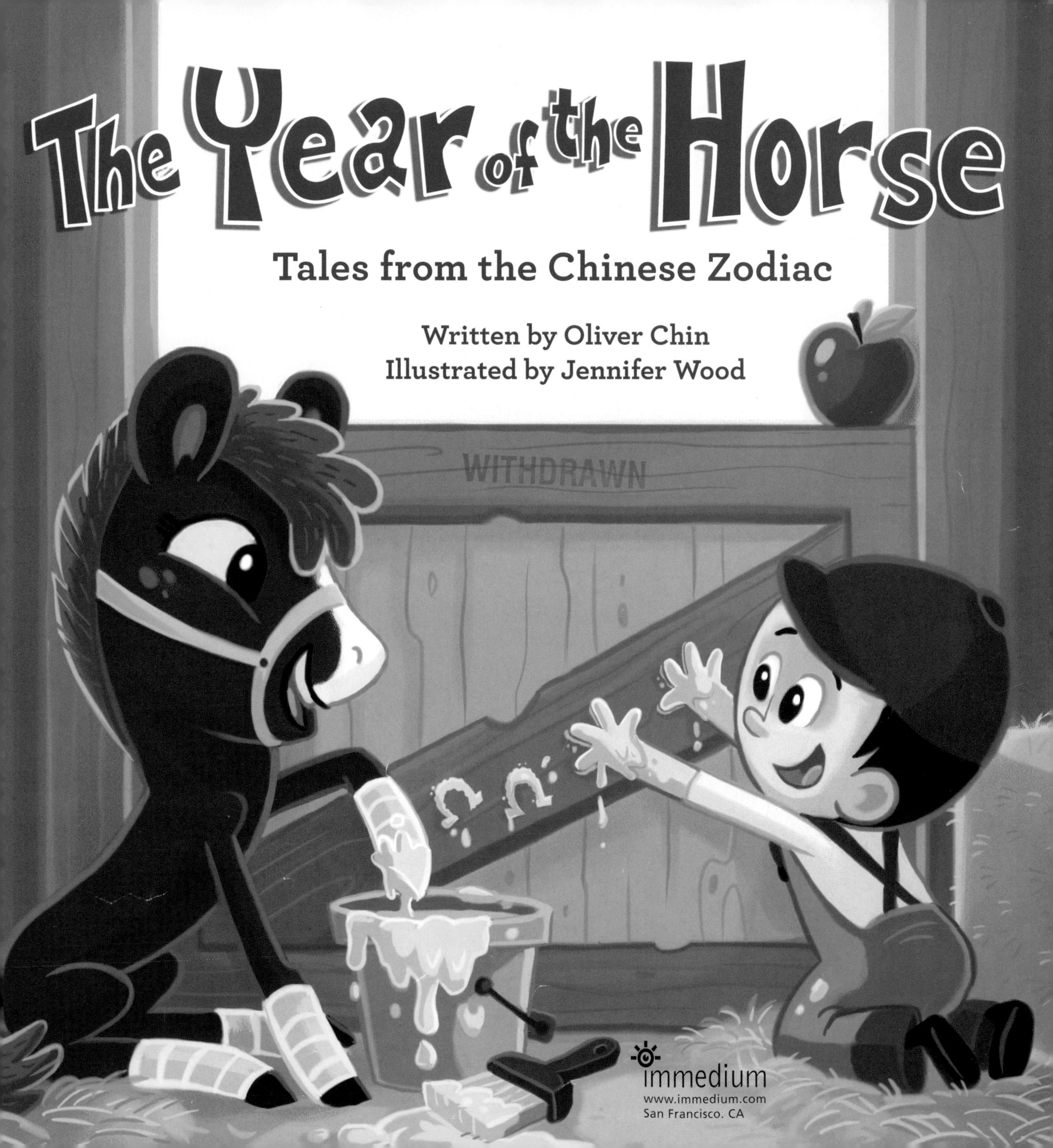
The Year of the Horse
Tales from the Chinese Zodiac
Written by Oliver Chin
Illustrated by Jennifer Wood
immedium
www.immedium.com
San Francisco, CA

After months of waiting, Mama and Papa horse finally welcomed their new baby. The foal tried to stand, wobbled, and gradually gained a sure footing. Her parents were thankful and named her "Hannah."

Their relatives came to congratulate them. "You've got yourselves a fine filly," remarked Uncle Fu.

Auntie Yee doted on her niece and added, "She already likes being the center of attention."

A teacher and her student were painting nearby and peeked into the stables. The boy remarked, "Lao Shi, this horse is as big as me!"

She laughed, "Ha! Tom, you are both very young and have a way to go."

Tom visited Hannah regularly, and soon they became friends. They liked to play games such as Roll Out The Barrel, Keep Away, and Musical Stalls.

Grazing in the pasture, Hannah daydreamed,
"I wonder what we'll be when we grow up?"

Papa answered, "Darling, we'll show you what we do."
So they followed the adults to the fairgrounds.

At the arena, Mama explained,
"Dear, I'm a show horse.
I train to jump hurdles
and trot gracefully."

Papa jogged at the fields. The stallion bragged,
"I'm a racehorse and run quickly around the track."

In town, they watched
Uncle Fu work.
He grunted,
"I'm a draft horse
and pull large
loads every day."

At the park,
they played with
Auntie Yee.
She said,
"I'm an old gray
mare and enjoy
being with kids."

Hannah admired her family,
"They have a lot of skills and responsibilities."

Grooming Hannah's velvet coat and combing her silky mane, Tom replied, "Hopefully, we'll find something that we're good at, too."

The next day a royal messenger delivered an important letter to Lao Shi.

She gasped, “The Governor has requested a new painting from me. But the capital is far away, and I cannot bring it there myself.”

"I'll help you, Lao Shi," volunteered Tom.

"The journey is too long and wild to walk alone," stated the teacher. "Someone must go with you."

So they set off to interview some candidates.

They found good prospects.
The sheep was an able hiker.
"But I provide the town's wool."

The dog was a loyal companion.
"But I guard the town's gate."

The ox was a strong worker.
"But I tend the town's farm."

As Tom and his teacher left empty-handed,
Hannah proposed, **"How about a horse?"**
Tom and Lao Shi liked her idea,
so they all went to ask her
family for their aid.

Her parents' ears perked up at the news. However, Papa remembered their schedule and shook his head. Mama neighed, "Unfortunately, our calendar is packed with many big contests."

Uncle Fu chewed the idea over, but sighed, "I'm sorry, but my workload is just too heavy as it is."

Auntie Yee politely declined, too. But she hinted, "I think you're looking for fresher legs than mine."

Hannah felt her friends' disappointment. Wanting to raise their hopes, Hannah piped up,

"I can do it!"

"Aren't you too young?" snorted Papa.

"Isn't the road too dangerous?" bridled Mama.

“But Hannah is becoming a big gal and has special qualities,” countered Lao Shi. They knew she was right and reluctantly agreed.

Tom and Hannah’s hearts raced. ***“THANK YOU!”*** they squealed in delight.

Now the horse and rider practiced together. Using gear and "giddy-ups," they patiently listened to each other and learned to act as one.

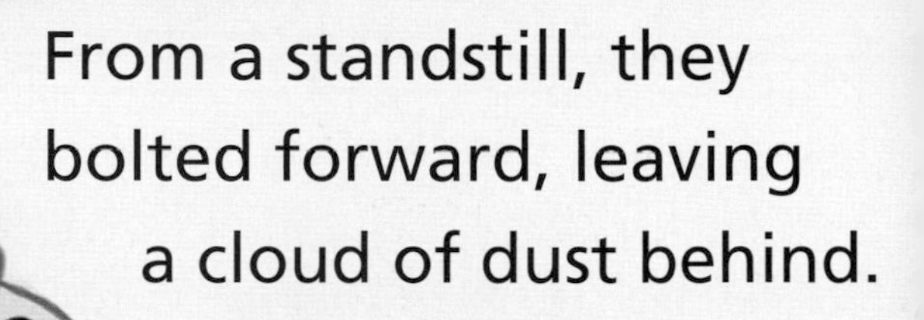

From a standstill, they bolted forward, leaving a cloud of dust behind.

Meanwhile, Lao Shi was inspired by their budding partnership. She drew big, broad strokes. She tried small, delicate brushes as well. Finally, after many sketches, she finished her painting with a satisfied smile.

Now it was time for Hannah and Tom's trip to begin.

Everyone gathered to say goodbye to the young travelers. With her art under wraps, Lao Shi advised, "Trust in each other and move as one."

Hannah's parents hugged her, "Dear, keep on the path and stay alert."

She assured them, **"I'll do my best, just like you taught me."** Tom took the reins and away they went.

The pair galloped across rolling hills and colorful meadows.

High in the saddle, Tom gazed in wonder as they passed towering peaks.

Hannah carried Tom as they crossed winding rivers. They were moving at a fast clip!

Then they entered a bamboo
forest and had to slowly
steer their way through
the shadows.

Suddenly Hannah heard a hiss,
halted in her tracks, and reared.
"Whoa!" yelled Tom. A snake lay
in their path!

But there was no room
to turn around. So Tom
spurred Hannah onward.
They charged ahead
and Hannah leapt high
over the hurdle.

"Good girl!"
praised Tom.

In the coming days, they would nimbly tiptoe past sleeping strangers.

During chilly nights, they kept warm below the soaring clouds that circled the misty mountains.

Shouldering Tom through sun and rain, Hannah would not halt. Finally, they glimpsed the capital, rising in the distance. Reaching their destination, they hollered, **"We made it!"**

They delivered Lao Shi's scroll to the grateful Governor. "Well done," he marveled and invited Tom and Hannah to dinner.

They rested and saw the city's sights, but were chomping at the bit to go home.

The Governor thanked Hannah and Tom and bid them farewell.

The return trip was more easygoing, as they stopped to admire the scenery and smell the flowers. At last, they happily arrived at their town gate.

The two received a rousing welcome.
"Hurray for Hannah!" shouted the crowd.
Lao Shi was glad to hear the Governor was so impressed that he wanted to start his own pony express. Then she gave them a present.

"Here is a copy of my painting," Lao Shi announced. "The word for horse stands for Hannah's valiant spirit."

Hannah's family pranced proudly and displayed the character prominently in the town square.

Afterward, Hannah and Tom continued to horse around.
They had fun counting their blessings and flicking their tails.
But they sincerely understood each other, as true teammates do.

These friends forged a strong bond
and blazed their own trail.
And everyone would always
celebrate this rewarding
Year of the Horse.

Horse

1918, 1930, 1942, 1954, 1966, 1978, 1990, 2002, 2014, 2026

People born in the Year of the Horse are energetic and animated. They are proud and love attention. But they can be impatient, hot-blooded, and headstrong. Though they are free spirits, horses are steadfast and resilient companions.